scribbling noted
1/9/23 - mm

writing noted CR 10/22

5/17

STICK CAT

STICK CAT

CAT

A tail of two kitties

By Tom Watson

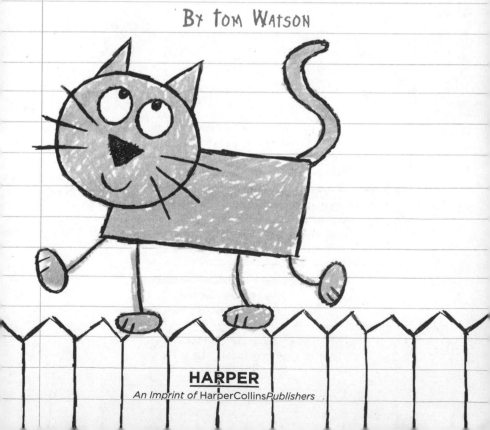

HARPER
An Imprint of HarperCollinsPublishers

to Mary, of course.
(SDLMM)

Stick Cat: A Tail of Two Kitties

Copyright © 2016 by Tom Watson

Illustrations by Ethan Long based on original sketches by Tom Watson

All rights reserved. Printed in the United States of America.

No part of this book may be used or reproduced in any manner whatsoever without written permission except in the case of brief quotations embodied in critical articles and reviews. For information address HarperCollins Children's Books, a division of HarperCollins Publishers, 195 Broadway, New York, NY 10007.

www.harpercollinschildrens.com

Library of Congress Control Number: 2015952521
ISBN 978-0-06-241100-6
ISBN 978-0-06-245716-5 (int.)

Typography by Jeff Shake

16 17 18 19 20   CG/RRDH   10 9 8 7 6 5

❖

First Edition

Table of Contents

Chapter 1

REMEMBER OUR DEAL?

Do you remember our deal from the Stick Dog books? You know, how you're *not* allowed to hassle me about my drawing skills and stuff? And how I *am* allowed to go off in other directions now and then?

I'm glad you remember, because I have a bit of a situation here. I need to go off in a *way* different direction.

And it's Mary's fault.

Who's Mary? Good question.

Let me just tell you how this all got started.

Mary Cunningham walked by my desk on the way to the pencil sharpener yesterday.

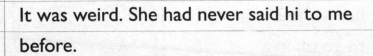

MARY

She paused for a second at my desk and said, "Hi."

It was weird. She had never said hi to me before.

It was right in the middle of Ms. Griffin's

English class. I was about to get cranking on a new Stick Dog story. It is pretty much my favorite part of every school day.

Mary sharpened her pencil and returned to her seat. One minute later the super-weird stuff began.

Mary came back.

This was her second trip to the pencil sharpener. Only this time she didn't just pause at my desk—she stopped. I know you probably think I'm making this up, but I'm not. I swear. She actually stopped.

Mary tapped her pencil on my composition book as she stood there right next to me. Her pencil has a little rubber cat eraser on it. It jiggled with each tap.

She has cat everything. Her folders and book covers have cats on them. She has cat sweaters and pencils and socks. I've noticed her talking a lot about her cats, Francis and Nora.

Can I tell you something weird? I don't know how it happened or when it happened, but something occurred last week or last month or whenever, and now girls are a lot less annoying and a lot more, you know, interesting.

And Mary is more interesting than any other girl in my class.

She stopped tapping her pencil and looked at me. The little orange-and-white cat eraser wobbled an extra couple of seconds after the pencil stopped moving. Mary stood real close on the left side of my desk.

It started to get warm in class for some reason.

I wondered if maybe Ms. Griffin should open a window.

"Are you working on another Stick Dog story?" Mary asked.

I nodded.

"What kind of food will they discover this time?"

"I'm thinking about candy," I answered. "A Halloween story maybe."

"That's a fun idea."

Okay, this was more than a walking-by-my-desk-on-the-way-to-the-pencil-sharpener comment. This was an official conversation.

I said, "I think it could be really funny if they follow two kids around the neighborhood on Halloween. And maybe they get all freaked out by the costumes and stuff."

That's when Mary did this really cool thing.

She laughed.

"You should do a story about cats," she suggested. "I have cats."

"Yeah, maybe." I didn't know what else to say.

"I'd like to read it if you do."

Then she left.

I only said one thing after Mary sat down at her desk again.

"Ms. Griffin," I called. "Can I open a window? It's really warm in here."

Chapter 2

STICK CAT AND GOOSE

Okay, this feline creature is going to need a name. I've thought about it for a very, very long time. And I've considered my own drawing abilities. I've chosen a name.

This is Stick Cat.

Stick Cat lives in an
apartment on the
twenty-third floor
of a big building in
the city. It's kind
of an old building.
Stick Cat has a
human roommate
named Goose.
I know, I know.
Goose is a very
strange name for a
human. But this is

STICK
CAT'S
APARTMENT

the only thing Stick Cat has ever heard his
roommate called. So that's that.

Between you and me, this guy has a neck
that looks a little out of proportion with his
head and the rest of his body. And my guess
is that somewhere back in grade school—

9

when it's really important to call people by anything *except* their real names—someone commented on his long neck, nicknamed him Goose, and now he's stuck with it.

That's just a guess. I don't know for sure.

Goose is not embarrassed by his name at all. In fact, he's embraced it. There are geese all around the apartment. He has goose pillows on the couch. He has a picture of geese flying above a field hung over the mantel in the living room. There is a neon sign in the kitchen that says "Goose Island Root Beer." It's really colorful, with lots of

orange and green tubular lights. Stick Cat
likes it during the day but can't stand how
much it glows at night if Goose forgets to
turn it off.

Goose works in the city. Every morning
during the week, Stick Cat watches Goose
eat his breakfast and brush his teeth. Then
Goose checks his pockets for his wallet,
keys, and phone, and walks over to where
Stick Cat is resting on the windowsill. This is
Stick Cat's favorite place.

It's where he can see another old building across the alley. That building is a lot like Stick Cat's, but instead of apartments, it has mainly businesses—an old piano factory is on a bunch of the upper floors. At street level, there is a piano store and a bakery. From this sill, he can also see the pigeons. There are dozens of pigeons that live in the alley and fly back and forth and perch on the window ledges of both buildings.

Anyway, this is where Stick Cat likes to sit the most—and it's where Goose comes every morning to do three things.

He opens the window a couple of inches so Stick Cat can feel a little breeze in his favorite spot.

Goose pats Stick Cat on the head.

Then he scratches him behind the left ear.

Stick Cat allows Goose to do all this. It's
how Stick Cat rewards Goose for working
all day and buying him food.

Then Goose says the same thing to Stick Cat
that he says every morning when he's about
to leave. He smiles and says, "Remember
to relax a little today." He says this in a
sarcastic way, like he knows that Stick Cat

is really going to sleep the entire day away. Then Goose gives Stick Cat a final scratch behind the ear—and leaves.

It's when Goose leaves that Stick Cat's day really gets started. And on this day, it all started with a single sound.

Stick Cat heard a scratching sound coming from the bathroom.

And Stick Cat knew who it was.

Chapter 3

EDITH

It was Edith.

Edith is the cat who lives in the apartment behind Stick Cat's. And Edith and Stick Cat get together every day when their human roommates go to work.

For months, you see, Edith would paw at her side of the wall, scratch at her side of the wall, and talk to Stick Cat from her side of the wall. And Stick Cat would paw, scratch, and talk back from his side of the wall.

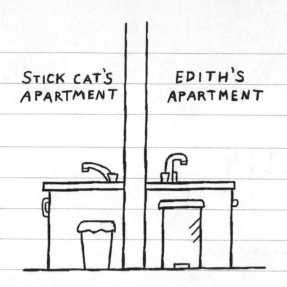

STICK CAT'S APARTMENT   EDITH'S APARTMENT

After all that pawing, scratching, and talking, they eventually found out where they could hear each other best. It was in the bathroom of each apartment. And the sink in each bathroom was built into the cabinet on opposite sides of that wall.

When their roommates are not around, it's through that wall that the two cats get together every day.

Edith climbs into the bathroom cabinet on

her side, scratches at the wall a couple of times, and pushes through a hole that they made together. Upon hearing the scratching signal, Stick Cat goes to the bathroom cabinet on his side and opens the door for her. To be perfectly honest, Edith could open the door herself, but she likes having it opened for her, and Stick Cat doesn't mind obliging her. It took them several weeks to scratch and claw at the wall inside the bathroom cabinets until they made a hole big enough for Edith to fit through. Although, on this day, Edith wasn't quite fitting.

"Stick Cat!" she called. "I'm stuck!"

Stick Cat dropped down from his windowsill perch. "Again?"

"Yes, again," Edith huffed. "Have you been making the hole smaller or something? I seem to get stuck a lot more often lately."

Stick Cat hustled across the carpet. He called, "How could I make a hole smaller? That's impossible."

"It's not impossible," Edith panted.

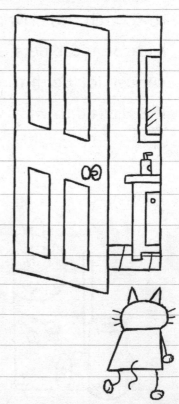

"Explain how," called Stick Cat. He was now halfway across the living room on his trip to the bathroom.

Edith huffed. You could tell by her voice that she didn't really want to have this debate with Stick Cat right now. What she wanted more than anything was to get unstuck. But she heard him padding his way nearer and nearer and figured she might as well try to get him to understand in the meantime.

"We scratched and dug into this wall for weeks to make this passageway, right?" she asked.

"Mm-hmm," Stick Cat answered as he walked into the bathroom.

"Well, then it makes perfectly good sense that to unmake the passageway, we would just do the opposite thing."

"Okaaay," Stick Cat answered slowly. "I'm

not quite following you, I guess. You can't unscratch something. Or undig something."

"Well, something is going on," Edith grunted in complaint. She was already willing to give up the argument. She was pretty uncomfortable. "I mean, I'm really jammed in here this time."

Even though her voice was muffled and she grunted a lot, Stick Cat could still make out what she said from inside the bathroom cabinet on his side of the wall.

"I'm coming."

When Stick Cat slid a claw under the edge
of the cabinet door, pulled it open, and
saw Edith, it was extremely difficult not to
laugh. There she was with only her head and
shoulders through the wall right next to the
sink pipe inside the bathroom cabinet.

"How did you . . . ?" he began to ask, but
then stopped himself.

"Let's not get all bogged down in how
or why this happened." Edith exhaled.
"Whether it was you making the hole
smaller or something else."

"Okay, let's not," Stick Cat agreed.

"Can we just get me out of here?"

Stick Cat nodded. "By 'we,' you mean 'me,' right? Because I don't really see how—in your present position—you're going to be able to assist with your own rescue."

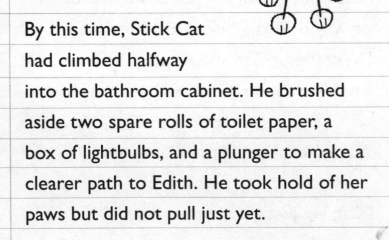

"It's not quite a *rescue*, Stick Cat. Let's not be too dramatic," Edith said, and pushed her two front legs straight toward him.

By this time, Stick Cat had climbed halfway into the bathroom cabinet. He brushed aside two spare rolls of toilet paper, a box of lightbulbs, and a plunger to make a clearer path to Edith. He took hold of her paws but did not pull just yet.

"If it's not a 'rescue,' then what would you call it?" Stick Cat asked.

"Just pull." Edith sighed.

"Seriously, we should have a better name for it, don't you think?" Stick Cat asked, still holding her paws but not pulling at all.

PULL.

"Just pull."

"How about if we call it feline dislodging?"

"Please pull."

"Emergency extraction?"

"Pull."

"Unplugging the kitty from the wall?"

Edith said nothing. Instead, she looked Stick Cat right in the eyes. Her left eye was squinted just slightly—but enough to let Stick Cat know that she had had enough.

Stick Cat pulled.

And Edith came tumbling out of her predicament. She rolled over Stick Cat and into the bathroom, scattering a few rolls of toilet paper onto the floor. Stick Cat pushed them back to the cabinet and placed them inside, nudging them over the bottom cabinet trim with his nose.

"Successfully unplugged," he said to her.

"Humph," Edith said, and gave her body a

quick shiver to get her fur properly aligned
across her body. With a couple of licks
and a quick examination in the long mirror
on the bathroom door, she found herself
presentable and strutted into the living
room.

Just by entering the
living room, Edith's
tension from being
stuck in the wall lifted.
She hopped up on
the couch and did
what she always did:
she turned the goose
pillows upside down
and pushed them into
the corner of the
couch. She really didn't
like those things.

"Don't you get sick of all these geese everywhere?"

Stick Cat had emerged from the bathroom as well.

"No, not really," Stick Cat said. "Goose likes them. And I like Goose. So they're fine with me."

"I think it's weird," Edith said as she jumped to the windowsill where Stick Cat had been perched just a few minutes before. She surveyed the streets below and the building directly across the alley. She noticed the clothesline outside. It stretched all the way across to the other building. Old Mrs. Maria O'Mahoney, a kindhearted Irish woman, lived in the apartment next door to Stick Cat's. And she had been drying her laundry this way for fifty-seven years. But only two things were on the line today: a yellow apron and a bag of clothespins. Those two things almost always hung there.

Stick Cat stretched, arching his back high in the air. It was as if he stretched the night's sleep out of his body. It was a gesture that meant he was ready to get started with the day. "What do you want to do? We can treasure hunt, listen to music, or play StareDown again."

Edith considered these options. "We played StareDown yesterday, didn't we?"

"Yes, we did."

StareDown was a game they played two or three times a week. It's sort of like how humans have a staring contest to try to see who blinks first. In the human version, the first one to blink loses. StareDown operates on similar principles. Stick Cat and Edith stare at each other for several minutes—but they are allowed to blink. In StareDown, the first one to fall asleep is the loser.

"Who won yesterday?" asked Edith.

"Don't you remember?"

"No," she answered.

"Why not?"

"I fell asleep, that's why," Edith said simply.

"Oh," Stick Cat said, and grinned to himself a bit. Edith didn't see him because she was still looking at the old building across the alley. "I don't remember either."

Edith moved her head back and forth to survey some of the piano factory's windows. "He's not there yet, so no music option," she commented, turning to Stick Cat. "We might as well go on a treasure hunt. Where do you want to start?"

"How about here?" asked Stick Cat. He dove beneath the couch before Edith could even answer. In just three seconds, she was under the couch with him.

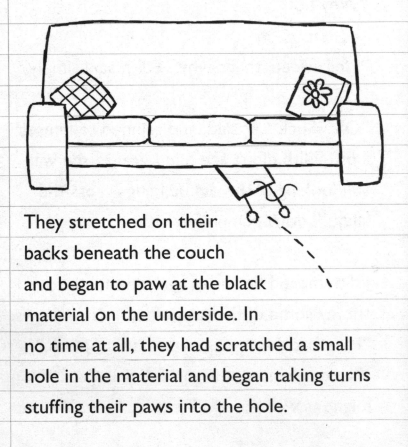

They stretched on their backs beneath the couch and began to paw at the black material on the underside. In no time at all, they had scratched a small hole in the material and began taking turns stuffing their paws into the hole.

On Edith's third turn, she yelled, "Treasure!"
and withdrew a shiny silver dime from the
hole.

"Whoa, that's a good one," Stick Cat said.
"What is it?"

Edith patted the dime back and forth with
her paws a few times while she considered
the question. "I'm pretty sure it's a lightbulb
of some kind. Even under here it has a shine
to it."

"A lightbulb?"

"Yes, that's right. A
lightbulb," Edith confirmed.
Now that she had made up
her mind about what the
object was, she grew more

and more confident about it.

"Don't lightbulbs only work in lamps?" Stick Cat asked. "Don't the lamps have to be plugged into the wall where those tiny holes are? You know—the holes that made your hair go all frizzy when you wanted to see what they tasted like?"

"Don't remind me," Edith whispered, and shook her head.

Sorry. Have to stop here. You know licking electrical outlets is a bad idea, right? I mean, really, really, really bad. Don't do it. Even if you want to have frizzy hair.

"A lightbulb, huh?" Stick Cat asked again. "It must have originally been in a lamp then, right?"

"Oh, I suppose so," Edith said. "The lamp is probably inside the couch too."

"You really think so?" Stick Cat asked. "Wouldn't Goose have noticed when he sat down that there was a big lamp stuck under the cushions?"

"Maybe he wouldn't," Edith tried to explain. "The whole thing is covered in those creepy goose pillows—maybe he didn't even notice."

Stick Cat just nodded his head, which was not very easy to do considering he was still under the couch. It was pretty easy to tell, however, that he didn't quite agree with Edith's lightbulb theory.

And Edith could tell too.

She responded, "Oh, very well. Do you want me to find the lamp in the couch?"

"I would love to watch that, yes."

For six minutes, Edith shoved her front paws into the hole in the bottom of the

couch. She pushed and stretched as far
as she could to the left. She pushed and
stretched as far as she could to the right.
Once, she reached so far to find a lamp in
the bottom of the couch that she pushed
her shoulders into the hole. For a moment,
Stick Cat was afraid he might have to unplug
her from the couch like he had unplugged
her from the wall earlier. Edith kept
muttering things like "I know it's in here
somewhere" and "If I could just reach a little
farther."

Stick Cat was about to ask her to stop
looking altogether. He was certain he had
seen some of these small silver circles before
when Goose emptied his pockets on the
kitchen counter after he got home from
work. And he was also pretty sure that
there was no way a lamp would fit into the

space at the bottom of the couch.

But he didn't have to stop Edith.

That's because right then the music started.

And when it did, Stick Cat and Edith
crawled out from under the couch and
sprinted across the carpet.

Stick Cat would soon hear the most
beautiful sound ever.

Chapter 4

MR. MUSIC

As soon as they heard the first notes played on the piano across the alley, Stick Cat and Edith raced to the windowsill. This was almost always the highlight of their day— and they never knew exactly when it would happen.

An old man with white frizzy hair worked in the piano factory across the alley. He wore overalls and carried a toolbox. The cats had named him Mr. Music. It was his job to keep all the pianos in tune—and there were a lot of pianos. You see, when a piano was sold in the store at street level, Mr. Music and another worker would pick out a new piano from these upper floors and bring it down a huge elevator to the store as a replacement. Keeping the pianos in tune and ready to sell was a big job.

Mr. Music had been doing it for years and years. As long as he could remember, Stick Cat had watched him— and listened to him—every day from that windowsill. The

MR. MUSIC

music provided a gentle and melodic accompaniment to all the city noises— talking people, car horns, sirens, and other things—that drifted up to the twenty-third floor from the street.

"Oh, he's close today!" Edith exclaimed, and placed her paws under the window's bottom edge.

Stick Cat did the same. Together, they pushed the window up much higher than Goose had left it to create an opening, about

twelve or fourteen inches high. They could hear the piano playing before, but now it came through even louder.

"He is really close today," Stick Cat confirmed.

This was typically not the case. With so many pianos to tune, it was rare that the cats could actually see Mr. Music. He was usually far away on another side of one of the floors. Perhaps once every two or three weeks was he where Stick Cat and Edith could see him. This time he was at the piano directly across from Stick Cat's window.

Now, even if Mr. Music was completely out of sight, the cats could still hear him play the piano. That's because he always opened several windows whenever he played. But today was the best combination of all: open windows and really, really close.

The cats settled in to listen.

Mr. Music followed the same routine with each piano he tuned. He played a few notes

and then opened his toolbox and set it on the
bench next to him. The box contained all
the things he needed to work on a piano—
and a package of Reese's Peanut Butter Cups
and a cell phone. Next, he opened the top
of the piano—today, it was a large, black
grand piano—and began to test each key.
He tilted his head a little as he listened. If he
didn't like the way a particular note sounded,
Mr. Music would double-check it
with a tuning fork and make an
adjustment to that key's
corresponding string
inside the piano.

It was when he finished testing the individual keys that the concert for the cats began.

He would put his tools back in the box, remove the box from the bench, and place it on the floor.

Mr. Music would then open the Reese's Cups and eat one— saving the other for after the concert. He would wipe his hands on his overalls, stretch his fingers, and begin to play.

Stick Cat and Edith watched as this series of events unfolded. It was early in the key testing that Mr. Music found the first off-key note.

T-wang! came a bad note from across the alley.

"Ouch," Edith said. She squeezed her eyes shut and scrunched her head down into her shoulders for a moment. "That was a clunker."

Stick Cat was used to these comments from Edith. She often provided play-by-play commentary during the piano tuning. With each off-key note, she almost always had something to say.

D-oink! came another bad note several minutes later.

"Yikes," Edith said, shaking her head in disgust. "Terrible, just terrible."

43

Sk-link!

"Please, please," she said, drawing her paws up over her ears. "Make it stop."

Thankfully for Edith, Mr. Music was, in fact, done. He put his tools away and opened his package of Reese's Cups.

"He's done, Edith," Stick Cat said loudly. He wanted to make sure that she could hear him through the paws over her ears. Stick Cat was just as thankful that Mr. Music was done tuning the grand piano. He didn't mind the sour notes that sounded out during the tuning process. It didn't last long— and he considered it a small price to pay, considering Mr. Music spent a good amount of time playing beautifully when the tuning was complete. It was Edith's comments about the tuning that he was happy to be done with. He said, "I always forget you have such a good ear for music."

Edith took this as a clear compliment. "Oh, yes, yes. It comes quite naturally to me. It's just a special talent I was born with," she said as she got herself into her favorite listening position now that the piano tuning was over. "My family is full of wonderful singers. Sometimes you can hear their beautiful songs in the middle of the night throughout the city. It's like music to my ears."

"You mean it *is* music to your ears."

"Hmm?"

"You mean it *is* music to your ears," Stick Cat said again. "The cats singing in the middle of the night. It *is* music. It's not *like* music."

"Oh, I suppose so," Edith answered. She appeared to be slightly put off. "If you have to be haughty about it."

"No, no. I didn't mean to cause offense," Stick Cat said, and shook his head. In truth, however, he had grown tired of Edith's attitude during the piano tuning. He had come to think of Mr. Music as a friend of sorts—someone who provided a beautiful interlude in Stick Cat's day. In some sense, Stick Cat felt he should defend him a bit. "Do *you* have this musical ability too? Like your family?"

"Of course," Edith answered immediately. "It's in my blood."

"Well, before he starts playing a song," suggested Stick Cat, "maybe you could sing a little bit right now."

Edith accepted this invitation with great enthusiasm. She went through a quick series of breathing exercises. She panted quickly for a few seconds and took several deep breaths. She coughed out a hair ball and panted a few more times.

"I would really rather warm up my voice a bit first," she said, and opened and closed her eyes a couple of times

HAIRBALL

47

rather slowly. "But with a voice like mine, the natural talents should shine through nonetheless."

All Stick Cat could think to say was "I'm sure that's true."

Edith sat up straight, inhaled, and began to sing.

She did not go into the job slowly or with ease. She did not build up to bigger, louder notes. She did not concern herself with developing a melody or a chorus. No, Edith did none of that.

Instead, she opened her mouth and began to sing as loud as she could. She thrust her right forepaw out high and in front of her—like an opera singer trying to project her voice as far as she could through physical force. While singing, Edith opened her eyes wide and looked at Stick Cat in a pleading, don't-you-think-I'm-a-wonderful-singer kind of way.

Stick Cat had never heard anything so terrible in his life.

The sound coming out of Edith's mouth was definitely not singing. It wasn't even close to singing. It was more like squealing. No, not squealing—more like screeching. Nope, nope, not even screeching. That doesn't do this ear-splitting sound enough justice.

Let's see, let's see. Okay, I think I got it.

Imagine this: A girl in your class with long fingernails is scratching a chalkboard repeatedly while screaming at the top of her lungs. Oh, yeah, there are also three dozen donkeys braying in the hallway while they stomp on harmonicas.

Can you imagine that?

Okay, now that you have imagined that, let me just say this: Edith's singing was worse—way worse.

And what could Stick Cat do? Nothing.

That's because while that terrible noise emitted from Edith's mouth, she kept staring at Stick Cat with that don't-you-think-I'm-a-wonderful-singer look.

For the next thirty seconds, Stick Cat smiled and nodded and used all his strength and willpower to resist slapping his paws over his ears.

There were other sounds all around them as Edith continued to, umm, sing. Cars honked and jackhammers rattled from the construction site around the corner. Stick Cat could also hear windows slam shut all around his apartment. Mrs. Maria O'Mahoney, the kindhearted Irish woman next door, yelled out her window, "Shush up, you old alley cat!" before slamming her window shut. Edith apparently didn't hear her though. She was perhaps too focused on—or maybe too deafened by—her, ahem, singing.

Then, finally, Mr. Music began to play his first song.

This made Edith stop singing. She wanted to listen too.

To Stick Cat, that combination—when Mr. Music *started* to play and Edith *stopped* singing—was the most beautiful sound ever.

What Stick Cat didn't know was that in a few minutes he would hear the worst sound ever.

Even worse than Edith's singing.

Chapter 5

ONE TERRIBLE MUSICAL NOTE

"Did you like my song?" Edith asked. She fell out of her opera-singing pose and settled back down on the windowsill.

Stick Cat positioned himself to listen to Mr. Music's piano playing as well. He curled himself almost into a circle and rested his chin on the sill. He didn't know quite how to answer.

"'Like' is not the right word," he said.

"'Admire'?" Edith asked. "Did you 'admire' my song?"

"That's not quite what I was thinking of either."

"'Adore'?" Edith asked. "Did you 'adore' my song?"

Stick Cat pressed his lips together tightly and shook his head.

"'Love'?"

"Those are all such wonderful words," Stick Cat said. "But even those words

LIKE?
ADMIRE?
ADORE?
LOVE?

can't accurately capture the feelings and sensations that your song brought out in me. I don't think any word could do your singing justice."

Edith didn't say anything at all for about twenty seconds. Stick Cat tried not to look at her, thinking his facial expression might give something away.

Finally, Edith spoke. "Stick Cat," she said. There was genuine emotion in her voice. "That's the most wonderful thing anyone has ever said to me. Thank you."

Stick Cat exhaled and said, "You're welcome."

And they settled in to listen to Mr. Music.

He usually played for ten or fifteen minutes
after he had finished tuning a particular
piano. And today was no different. Stick
Cat wasn't quite sure, to be honest,
whether Mr. Music's playing was just the
final test of the piano's tunefulness—or if
it was just how he took a break after each
job.

It didn't matter, of course, to Stick Cat. The
songs Mr. Music played poured out through
the open windows and drifted sweetly
across the
alley to where
he and Edith
simply listened
and enjoyed
them.

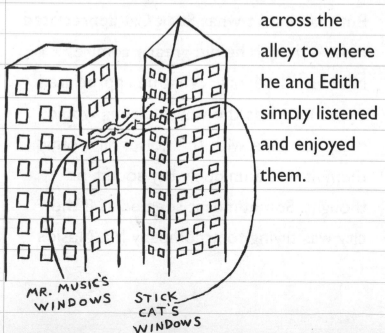

MR. MUSIC'S
WINDOWS

STICK
CAT'S
WINDOWS

Mr. Music had a style of playing that allowed the notes to begin slowly, rolling in rhythm out in the air. Then, in the middle of a piece, the pace would quicken, and a deeper sub-sound would serve as a sort of background to the song. Finally, in the closing minute or two of each tune, Mr. Music's frizzy white hair would begin to shake and bounce. His shoulders would jerk up and down a bit. The piano notes would come in a final flourish and then fade slowly and quietly away.

But that wasn't what Stick Cat appreciated most—though he did greatly admire Mr. Music's talents. What he appreciated even more was the way the song would often combine with the noises all around them. It was a uniquely *city* sound, he thought. Sometimes it seemed as if the city was trying to accompany Mr. Music's

song. The clattering of an old taxicab, or
a traffic policeman blowing a whistle, or
groups of cars accelerating and decelerating
at stoplights often seemed to work with the
rhythm of the song.

And sometimes, Stick Cat thought, it
was the other way around. Sometimes it
seemed that Mr. Music played music to blend
rhythmically with the beats of the city.

Today, two sounds from
the construction site down
on the street seemed
to work in conjunction
with Mr. Music's song:
a jackhammer and the
beeping of a cement truck
as it backed down the alley.

BEEP! BEEP! BEEP!

It all worked together beautifully as
Mr. Music finished the concert.

Edith sighed in satisfaction. "It was almost
as good as my singing," she commented.

Stick Cat did not say anything but did watch
as Mr. Music finished his routine at the
piano. Stick Cat knew what Mr. Music would
do now. He would stand up and stretch. He
would lean forward and close the piano lid.
And then Mr. Music would sit back down on
the bench, eat the second Reese's Cup, and
make a phone call.

Stick Cat watched him stand up and stretch his arms above his head and spread his fingers wide. Mr. Music held that position for a few seconds and then leaned forward to close the piano lid.

Stick Cat glanced down at the cement truck in the alley.

It continued to back up and beep—and gain speed. It was going way too fast. Stick Cat had seen plenty of trucks from his window, and whenever they backed up, they always went slowly and made that beeping sound.

But not this cement truck.

Something was wrong.

The truck slammed into a light pole and a car that was parked in the alley. It took a second for the tremendous, metallic *CRASH!* to travel up to the twenty-third floor where Stick Cat and Edith could hear it. And it took another second for the vibration of the impact to travel up to them. It shook the building.

They both grabbed on to the sill to keep their balance. As they did, another huge and horrible sound erupted.

It was as if all the bad musical notes a piano could make were played all at once. It was one thunderous crack of sound—one terrible musical note. It seemed to echo and shake in the air.

Stick Cat looked across the alley at the piano factory.

Mr. Music stood awkwardly there at the piano.

And he wasn't moving.

Chapter 6

IT WAS THUNDER

Stick Cat could tell instantly what had happened.

Mr. Music's arms were stuck in the piano.

The vibration from the cement truck crash had jarred the building across the alley too—and the piano lid shook loose from its prop and smashed down just as Mr. Music reached inside to close it himself. When the lid smashed, that awful combination of musical notes had erupted from the piano.

Looking closer, Stick Cat could now see that Mr. Music was in fact moving a little. He tried to pull his arms free, but it was clear the lid was far too heavy.

He was trapped.

Stick Cat saw him turn his head and look down at the toolbox on the floor next to the bench. His cell phone was there next to the remaining Reese's Cup—they had both been jostled off the bench when the building shook. Mr. Music tried to pull the phone closer with his foot, but it was at least three feet out of reach. He kept wriggling his arms, shoulders, hips, and legs, trying to find some kind of position that could help him escape.

It was then that Edith spoke up.

"What's he dancing for?" she asked. "Doesn't he know the music's over?"

Stick Cat turned to look at her.

"I mean," she continued, "he was the one playing the music. You'd think he'd know that it stopped. You know what I mean?"

"Umm," said Stick Cat. He needed to explain things to Edith and then try to see if there was something he could do to help. "I'm pretty sure he's not dancing. I think his arms might be stuck in the piano. I think the lid might have come down when he wasn't expecting it."

"How could that have happened?" Edith tilted her head and looked across the alley at Mr. Music again. "Do you think it's like a monster piano or something?"

"No-o-o," answered Stick Cat slowly. "I don't think it is a monster piano. I think maybe when that cement truck crashed down in the alley a minute ago that—"

"What cement truck?" interrupted Edith. "What crash?!"

Stick Cat held very still for a moment. He really wanted this to be over with. "Umm," he finally said, and pointed to the alley. "You know that loud sound we heard a minute ago and then the building vibrated? It was that cement truck down there. It smashed into a light pole and a parked car."

Edith cast a doubtful glance down to the alley.

"I think that was thunder, Stick Cat."

Stick Cat looked up. Despite being surrounded by some pretty tall buildings, he had a fairly good view of the sky. It was clear and blue—not a cloud anywhere. "Thunder?" he asked.

"Thunder. That's what it was."

"Do you see the wrecked cement truck down there?"

"I think it's just parked."

"Just parked?"

"That's right, just parked."

Stick Cat resisted shaking his head. "But do

you see the smashed car down there? It's all crumpled up. And the streetlight lying in the street?"

"People in this city will park anywhere," Edith said matter-of-factly.

"And do you hear the police sirens?" Stick Cat asked. "They're getting closer. They're probably coming because of the wreck. That's what police do."

"They could be going anywhere," Edith answered, refusing to concede any of this to Stick Cat. "Maybe they're investigating the damage done by that ferocious thunder."

He looked across the alley and into the piano factory before speaking again. Mr. Music was in the exact same position. He had tried to sit back down on the bench, but he couldn't bend far enough with his arms caught in the piano. He was clearly growing more and more uncomfortable. When Stick Cat saw just how trapped Mr. Music was, he became convinced that he must do something to help.

He turned immediately to Edith and looked her right in the eyes. "Edith," he said. "You're absolutely right. People in this city park against wrecked cars and over broken streetlights all the time. And I'm sure that what we heard was thunder too. I don't know why I didn't think of that before."

"Sometimes, Stick Cat," said Edith, and then she paused for a few seconds. "Sometimes, I think you get lost in your own little world—never even aware of the things going on around you. It's okay—lots of cats are like that. I'm not one of them—but there's nothing wrong with it. So you didn't recognize the thunder, no big deal. Take it easy on yourself."

"I'll do that," Stick Cat said, and nodded his head. "That thunderclap you heard seems to have rattled the building across the street and trapped Mr. Music in the piano. I really want to help him. But I don't know how to get over there."

"I have an idea," Edith said. She seemed
to have grown more confident both in her
stature and in her voice since Stick Cat had
admitted the big sound was thunder.

TAP
TAP
TAP

"That's great!" Stick Cat exclaimed.

"Yes, yes. No need to worry," Edith answered, and casually hopped down.

"Where are you going?" Stick Cat asked.

"To the bathroom."

"Why?"

"I need to check the fur on my back leg in the mirror," explained Edith. She kind

of stuck her hip out a bit to demonstrate
where she meant. "It's sticking up a bit."

"Can't that wait?"
Stick Cat asked quickly.

"I don't like walking
around when I don't
look my best," Edith
answered.

Stick Cat glanced
across the alley again. Mr. Music was
in the exact same position: stuck and
uncomfortable. Stick Cat had to hurry.
He had to find a way. "Maybe you could
look in the mirror after we've figured out
a way to help Mr. Music," he said. Then he
immediately added, "I think that area of fur
looks really nice actually. It's quite clean and

has a wonderful sheen to it."

"Thank you," answered Edith. She stopped and glanced down at herself. "Thank you very much."

"Now, about that idea to get across the alley to save Mr. Music?" Stick Cat asked, happy to have stopped this delay. "What is it?"

Edith cocked her head sideways a bit and looked at Stick Cat curiously. It was as if she couldn't understand how Stick Cat hadn't thought of her idea himself. "It's easy," she said. "We fly."

"Fly?"

"Yes, fly," Edith said. You could tell that she wasn't quite sure if Stick Cat knew what she was talking about. So, to demonstrate, Edith began to hop up and down on her back paws and flap her arms. "You know, fly! Like this!"

Stick Cat stared at Edith in wonder. After a moment, he said, "You know you're not flying, right?"

"Of course, silly," Edith panted. She was already tired from hopping and flapping. "I just wanted you to know what flying is."

"I *know* what flying is," answered Stick Cat. He tried not to sound exasperated even though he definitely felt that way. "I also know that cats can't fly. We don't have wings."

"Oh, don't get so caught up in the details," Edith said.

Stick Cat stopped talking. He lowered his head for a moment and looked at the living-room carpet. He tried to think of all the things that calmed him down: when he sat on the couch next to Goose and allowed him to stroke his back, the slow and melodic beginnings to all of Mr. Music's songs, Edith's soft pattern of breathing when she was asleep on the windowsill after a game of StareDown.

Finally, he lifted his head and calmly said, "It's an excellent idea you've come up with. I wish we could fly, Edith. It would be a great plan. But we don't have wings."

"I know that, Mister Fluffy Pants," she

said, and giggled. "We just need to borrow some."

"Borrow some?"

"That's right," answered Edith as she climbed back up next to Stick Cat. "From the pigeons. There are dozens of them out here every day."

"You want to borrow the pigeons' wings and attach them to ourselves somehow?" asked

Stick Cat. He was not being impolite. He just wanted to understand what Edith was talking about. There were certainly times in the past when he thought Edith might not have, umm, all her whiskers in the right place, if you know what I mean. But he certainly didn't believe Edith would consider taking the wings off a couple of pigeons and reattaching them somehow to themselves to fly across the alley. Even for Edith, this idea seemed a little bizarre.

Thankfully, this is not what she was thinking about doing.

She turned directly toward him, lowered her chin, and raised her eyes. "Stick Cat, seriously. How could you even think such a thing?"

"*I* didn't think such a thing," he responded quickly. "I just wanted to make sure that *you* weren't thinking such a thing."

"I'm not," Edith answered, slightly offended. "I would never suggest such a crazy idea. I mean, really, Stick Cat. Sometimes I wonder about you."

Stick Cat raised both of his front paws, pads out, toward Edith. "I'm sorry," he said sincerely. "It's just all these things going on. The truck crash—I mean, the thunder— and that loud, banging musical note and Mr. Music being trapped. We were relaxing so nicely and listening to the music, and then everything changed instantly. I'm just not thinking straight probably."

"It's okay, Stick Cat. Why don't you just let me take it from here since you're all out of sorts."

"Okay," Stick Cat said. He took several calming breaths, inhaling and exhaling slowly and purposefully. "Tell me then, Edith. What do you mean by 'flying'?"

"First, we wait for a couple of pigeons to fly by. Second, we get ready to jump," Edith said, and straightened her posture on the windowsill. She rocked back on her hind legs a bit to demonstrate. "Then when they get right in front of the window, we jump! We grab hold of their legs and fly across that way."

Stick Cat could not say anything. For an instant, he wondered if, in fact, tearing off some pigeon wings and reattaching them to themselves might actually work better than this flying idea that Edith had just proposed. He knew the pigeons—and Edith and himself—would immediately plummet to the street from the twenty-third floor. And that was assuming a couple of pigeons happened to fly by his window, they timed their jumps perfectly, and they managed to hold on to the pigeons' legs.

"It's great, isn't it?" Edith asked. She had that look on her face from earlier when she was, umm, singing.

Stick Cat looked across the alley and through the windows of the old piano factory. Mr. Music hadn't moved.

Occasionally, he would turn his head, and Stick Cat could see that his face was red and flushed. It was quite obvious that Mr. Music was in a good bit of trouble— and a good bit of pain.

Stick Cat knew he had two problems to deal with. He had to figure out a way to reject Edith's plan. And he had to come up with a plan of his own.

He dealt with the first problem first—but probably not in the way that you might think.

Stick Cat looked away from Mr. Music and directly at Edith.

He said, "It's a brilliant plan. Let's do it."

Chapter 7

CATNAP

Stick Cat stretched a little and crouched right next to Edith. He too drew his weight back on his hind legs in a poised-and-ready-to-jump position.

"Does this look right?" he asked Edith.

She glanced at him and nodded.

"So when some pigeons fly by, we jump and grab their legs, right?"

"That's right."

"And then they fly us over to the piano factory?"

"Right."

"Got it," Stick Cat said with absolute conviction. He pushed off with his back feet just a bit—as if practicing his takeoff for the exact moment when a pigeon would fly by. Edith saw this, thought it looked like a good idea, and began pushing off a bit too. "There are bound to be a couple of pigeons any minute."

Now, there are a couple of things that Stick Cat knows that you and I don't. And knowing those things was all part of his plan. Here are the two things Stick Cat knew:

1. When there are two cats sitting on a windowsill, pigeons don't fly anywhere near them.

Cats and birds, you see, do not get along typically. In fact, birds are quite scared of cats because they know this: cats like to catch birds and eat them. Good reason to be afraid of them, right?

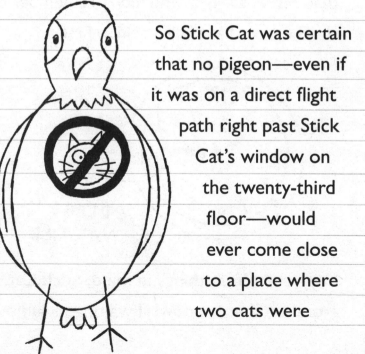

So Stick Cat was certain that no pigeon—even if it was on a direct flight path right past Stick Cat's window on the twenty-third floor—would ever come close to a place where two cats were poised in a ready-to-jump position.

2. It was almost Edith's nap time.
Stick Cat knew that Edith always fell asleep midmorning. In fact, he often proposed StareDown games at just this time. It was fun to watch Edith try to stay awake when she really wanted to win. Of course, Stick Cat almost always won—but he didn't tell Edith that. He'd usually say he didn't remember or that he must have fallen asleep first.

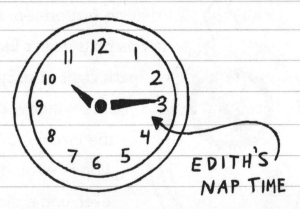

EDITH'S
NAP TIME

With these two things in mind, Stick Cat stood on that windowsill waiting to jump—

even though he knew he would never get the opportunity—and waiting for Edith to fall asleep.

As he waited, he watched Mr. Music attempt to free his arms from the piano two more times. He tried to pull his right shoulder back and his left shoulder back, but his arms remained firmly trapped under the grand piano's heavy lid.

Stick Cat wondered if Edith was asleep. He didn't want to look just yet. He didn't want to spark a conversation that might keep her awake a few minutes longer. So he waited for one minute.

And then one minute more.

Stick Cat was debating whether to wait one

additional minute when he heard a very familiar sound.

Edith was snoring.

HAVNK-SHOO...
...HAVNK-SHOO...
...HAVNK-SHOO...

While she slept, Stick Cat began to devise his own plan to get across the alley to save Mr. Music. After allowing Edith to sleep for five minutes, Stick Cat tapped her on the shoulder and said, "Edith, time to wake up."

She woke right up, refreshed from her nap. She stretched, looked around, and asked,

"How long have I been asleep?"

"I'm not sure," said Stick Cat. "Maybe an hour or so."

Edith licked her paws, ensuring that each strand of fur was again properly aligned. When she was done, she asked, "Did you fly across the alley hanging on to a pigeon?"

"No," answered Stick Cat slowly. "A few pigeons came really close, but not close enough to jump. But I don't think we have any more time to wait. We really have to get over there and help Mr. Music."

"It's just a darn shame we can't use such an excellent plan," Edith said.

"You're right about that," Stick Cat said. "But I think I may have come up with another idea."

"Is it a good idea?" Edith asked.

"It's okay, I guess."

"Is it as good as jumping off the ledge, grabbing two pigeons by the feet, and flying across the alley?"

Stick Cat shook his head as sincerely as he could. "No, no. It's not as good as that. Not even close."

"Well, what is it then?"

"I'll tell you, but first I have to ask you one question," Stick Cat said, and glanced past Edith along the outside of their building. "How do you look in yellow?"

"How do I look in yellow?" Edith repeated. "What kind of question is that? I mean, I suppose I'd look very good in yellow. But it's such an odd question."

"Why?" Stick Cat asked.

"Well, because I'm sure I'd look good in any color, that's why," Edith explained. She then puffed out her chest a bit and took a quick accounting of her appearance. After several seconds and a couple of primping licks, she added, "Yes, for someone like me, the color really makes no difference."

"Good," said Stick Cat. "Because we're going to play dress-up."

"With human clothes?" asked Edith. She began to get excited. You could tell she thought this idea might be fun. "With Goose's clothes? We tried that once before, remember? But we never got to the actual dressing-up part. Why was that?"

Stick Cat remembered. "His socks were all rolled up into balls," he recollected. "And we just ended up batting them back and forth for a few hours."

"We did?"

"We're cats." Stick Cat shrugged. "We couldn't help ourselves."

This made perfectly good sense to Edith, who nodded and then asked, "So, we're using Goose's clothes but avoiding the sock drawer?"

Stick Cat shook his head.

"What are we going to dress up in then?"

"That," Stick Cat said, and pointed past Edith

toward Mrs. O'Mahoney's window next door. The clothesline was attached to the brick wall near the window with a strong metal clip.

Two things—a bag of wooden clothespins and a yellow apron—were tied to the line. Mrs. O'Mahoney pulled the apron in whenever she baked bread or biscuits and put it back out when she was done. She liked to let the breeze blow the powdery flour off it. And Stick Cat liked to watch the little puffs of white flour escape into the wind.

"Yuck," Edith said immediately. "I'm not wearing that thing. It's too old-fashioned. I have a more modern sense of style than that."

Now, you've probably already guessed what Stick Cat's plan is all about. He and Edith would climb into the pocket of that apron hanging on his neighbor's line. Then they would move across the narrow alley by pulling on the opposite line. He had seen Mrs. O'Mahoney put out and take in laundry hundreds of times, and he was certain he knew how the clothesline worked.

The problem was, he didn't think he could convince Edith to do it. That's where the whole playing-dress-up idea came from. He thought she might enjoy dressing up enough that she wouldn't notice they were traversing their way across the alley twenty-three floors above street level.

But apparently that wasn't going to work, Stick Cat now knew.

"It's way too big for me anyway, Stick Cat," Edith said. Then she turned to him quickly and tilted her head slightly. "You don't think I'm fat, do you?"

Stick Cat knew this was dangerous territory to tread. Quickly, he said, "Of course not! In fact, I was about to ask if you've been working out. You look so healthy and trim lately."

This eased Edith's mood immediately. "Well, maybe I have, and maybe I haven't," she said coyly. "That's just for me to know and you to find out."

Having averted the do-you-think-I'm-fat crisis, Stick Cat tried a different approach.

"My plan isn't really about playing dress-up anyway," he said. "We were just going to ride across that clothesline in that yellow apron's pocket."

"Ride over in the pocket?!"

"Yes."

"Twenty-three floors above the street!?"

"Yes," Stick Cat said slowly. He was already pondering an alternative way for them to get over to help Mr. Music.

And as he was thinking, Edith said, "That sounds like a blast! Let's do it!"

And with that, Edith did the most confounded and amazing thing Stick Cat had ever seen.

She jumped.

Chapter 8

"GET YOUR TAIL OVER HERE"

Before Stick Cat could say or do anything, Edith had landed on Mrs. O'Mahoney's window ledge. She had simply, and without hesitation, pivoted on her paws when she was on Stick Cat's window ledge and leaped the four or five feet to the ledge next door.

"Are you crazy?!" Stick Cat yelled. He was truly astonished at what he had just witnessed. "You did that without even thinking about it!"

"Did what?" asked Edith casually.

"You jumped across to my neighbor's window ledge!" he yelled. And then, as if to explain things further, he added, "We're twenty-three floors up!"

Edith checked her reflection in Mrs. O'Mahoney's kitchen window. After a few seconds, she looked away from the window and back toward Stick Cat. She seemed satisfied with her appearance. "And what's your point?"

"My point!?" exclaimed Stick Cat. "Well, my point is, it's extremely dangerous. That's my point!"

"It's dangerous?"

Stick Cat shook his head—more to himself out of sheer amazement than anything else. He looked over to Edith on the next ledge and said, "Let me ask you something. Would you jump off a bridge if all your friends were doing it?"

"You bet I would!" Edith answered without pausing for a solitary moment. "That sounds like fun!"

WHEE!

"You would?!"

"Absolutely!"

"But—" and then Stick Cat stopped talking.

This gave Edith a chance to ask a couple of questions herself. "When do we go? Where's the bridge? Is it far from here?"

Stick Cat looked across the alley toward Mr. Music. He had to get over to his neighbor's ledge, ride across the alley in the apron with Edith, and then figure out how to get Mr. Music untrapped from that piano.

"We're not going," he said to Edith. "It's just a rhetorical question."

"You mean, there's no bridge? We're not going to jump?"

"No, not today," Stick Cat said.

"Bummer," Edith muttered. She seemed honestly disappointed. Then her voice picked up a bit, and she asked, "Maybe tomorrow? Or maybe some other day?"

"Umm, sure," Stick Cat answered. He was beginning to contemplate the jump from his ledge to Mrs. O'Mahoney's. "I guess."

This seemed to satisfy Edith enough for the time being. Stick Cat, meanwhile, tried to determine if he should push off with two legs or four legs. And he calculated how much room he would need to slide and stop himself.

"Well, what are you waiting for?" asked Edith. She had backed to the far corner of Mrs. O'Mahoney's ledge now and motioned for Stick Cat to jump. "Get your tail over here."

There was something in the way she said it that made Stick Cat jump. It was as if there was no doubt that he would make it. It was just an accepted fact. She had complete faith that he could do it. And this instilled a great deal of confidence in Stick Cat himself.

Without looking down, he jumped. He pushed off with his back legs, stretched his body long, and kept an eye on his target area. He landed with all four paws on the nearest part of that concrete ledge and then slid across before bumping a bit into Edith.

"Careful there, buster," she said, and pushed him back a smidgeon. She licked herself where they had made contact. "You're going to mess up the way my fur is lying."

"Sorry," Stick Cat said.

He looked into the neighbor's window and was happy to see that Mrs. O'Mahoney wasn't in the kitchen. Comfortable with that fact, Stick Cat turned to look at the apron on the clothesline. It was a few feet out, and just a little farther was a bag of wooden clothespins. Thankfully, the line was within easy reach, and he could reel the apron right up to the ledge. He was about to do so when Edith spoke.

"So, we need to hop into that apron? Into the pocket? To ride across?"

"That's right. We need to—"

But before Stick Cat could finish his sentence—or even finish his thought— Edith leaped from the ledge and dove into the pocket of the yellow apron.

It happened so quickly that Stick Cat wasn't even sure Edith had made it into her intended target. He was afraid to look down—afraid he might see Edith plummeting to her doom.

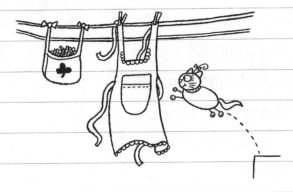

Instead, he stared at the apron. It moved and jostled, but Stick Cat couldn't tell if it was caused by the wind blowing—or by Edith squiggling around in the pocket.

He waited.

It was only a few seconds, but it felt much longer than that.

Edith poked her head out of the pocket,

stroked the fur on her left cheek, and
smiled at him.

"Stop doing that!" Stick
Cat exclaimed. He
reached out to the line
and began to reel the
apron closer. He shook
his head.

"Stop doing what?"

"Just jumping and doing dangerous stuff
without even thinking about it." Stick Cat
sighed. "I was still talking when you jumped.
It scared me like crazy."

As Stick Cat pulled the apron closer, it
began to swing, and Edith clearly enjoyed
the motion. She began to rock her body

back and forth in the pocket to magnify the swinging effect.

"Whee!" she yelled. "Swing me harder, Stick Cat!"

Stick Cat did change his reeling technique. He pulled the line a little faster. He wanted to get into that pocket and calm Edith down. And he wanted to get across to Mr. Music. He still wasn't sure how he would help him once—if—they got across.

When the apron brushed up against the ledge, Edith stopped swinging back and forth, and Stick Cat climbed into the pocket, digging his front claws into the cotton material for a very good grip. After securing himself in the pocket and waiting for the apron to balance out, he slowly stretched his head out enough to see.

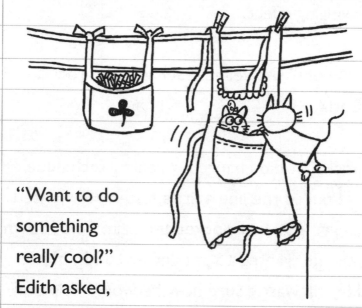

"Want to do
something
really cool?"
Edith asked,
staring right at him. She was clearly more
comfortable being twenty-three floors up in
the air than Stick Cat was.

"Like what?"

"If you lean your head out and look straight
down to the ground, it makes your stomach
feel like it's upside down or something. It's a

really funny feeling!"

Stick Cat nodded.

"Go ahead," Edith encouraged. "Try it!"

"No thanks."

"Come on. It won't kill you to try it."

"I'm not sure that's entirely true," Stick Cat whispered. Edith didn't hear him though.

"Come on. Just one peek!"

Stick Cat leaned his head out and over the edge of the pocket and looked downward. Edith was exactly right: it did make his stomach feel like it was upside down.

It was not a good feeling.

He quickly pulled his head back into the pocket.

"Neat, isn't it?" Edith asked.

Stick Cat emerged a bit and nodded his head nervously. He managed to get his body as secure as he could in the bottom of the pocket and stretched his front legs out to reach the other clothesline. It was made of rope, and he could easily press his claws into the braids to make it move.

And that's exactly what he did. He wanted to get across the alley—and out of this apron—as quickly as possible.

It took approximately two minutes to get

all the way across.

Edith enjoyed the trip immensely. She looked
down to the alley several times and giggled
and talked about how funny her stomach
felt. She shifted her weight back and forth
to make the apron swing on the line. To
satisfy her curiosity, she stretched out of the
pocket to look into the bag of clothespins
that hung next to the apron.

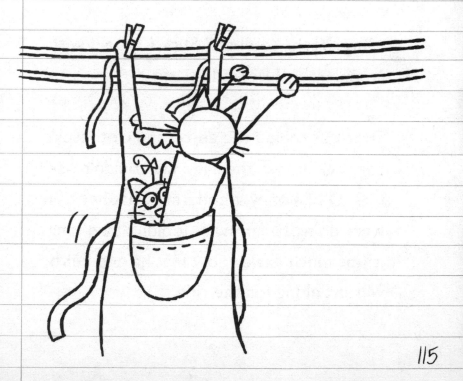

When they got to the piano factory window, Edith hopped out to the ledge. Stick Cat maneuvered the apron as close to the window as possible and climbed out too.

Edith looked back across at the way they had come. It was as if she was remembering every second of the trip as she looked. "That was awesome," she said. "I can't wait to do it again. How about you?"

"Sure. Yeah. You bet," Stick Cat said with considerably less enthusiasm.

Stick Cat reeled the apron and clothespin bag back across the alley. He couldn't risk Mrs. O'Mahoney wondering what her things were doing so far away. It didn't take long— it was much easier now that he and Edith weren't along for the ride.

When he was finished, Stick Cat jumped down from the ledge and onto the piano factory floor. He was so happy to have something firm and still under his paws.

He turned his head to see Mr. Music with his arms still stuck in that piano.

And Mr. Music stared right back at Stick Cat.

Chapter 9

P-H-A-T

Mr. Music appeared quite startled to see Stick Cat and Edith come through the open window. But in an instant he recovered from the surprise and called to them both, "Here, kitties!"

Stick Cat hurried to Mr. Music and rubbed up against his pants legs to demonstrate that he was a friend and there to help.

"You're a nice one," Mr. Music said. He rolled his shoulders and lifted his feet off the ground in turn, attempting to keep the blood flowing through his body. He had been in this position for some time and had grown quite stiff. He looked down at Stick Cat and said, "My arms are stuck in this darn piano, and I can't get them out. I don't know what happened. There was a big crashing sound and then the piano lid slammed down onto my arms."

"It was thunder," Edith said as she came closer too. Of course, Mr. Music couldn't understand her, but she felt obliged to explain what happened all the same.

"I used to have a cat," Mr. Music said, and glanced up at the ceiling. It was decorated with tin tiles that seemed to catch and reflect all the light in the room. "His name was Felix. He was almost all black but had white fur on his paws. Felix and I used to love to read the paper in the morning and watch the evening news together. He was quite up to date on current events."

Stick Cat liked the sound of Mr. Music's voice—almost as much as he liked the sound of Mr. Music playing the piano. There was a certain serenity in his voice. And it was easy to tell that he missed Felix very much. Not in a sad way, but more in a happy and memorable way.

Stick Cat was even more determined to help Mr. Music out of his predicament.

He jumped to the piano bench, sprang to the side of the keys, and then walked across the top shelf of the piano above the keyboard. He carefully stepped over and between Mr. Music's arms.

"Coming closer, are you?" whispered Mr. Music. "Well, you're a brave boy, I can tell. I could use the company. Usually my songs keep me company. But I can't exactly play right now."

Stick Cat paused, looked at him, and purred, but he did not stop. He kept moving past until he reached the open crack of the piano top. He could see that it had several hinges. He flattened himself as much as he could and stuck his head and shoulders inside the piano to investigate and try to devise a rescue plan. He could see Mr. Music's elbows, forearms, and hands inside the piano. They were smashed tightly between the lid and some cross braces inside. There

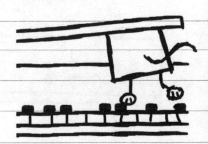

was absolutely no wiggle room.

Stick Cat knew he would have to lift the piano lid. If he could move it a few inches somehow, Mr. Music might have just enough space to wriggle free.

With his head and shoulders inside the piano, Stick Cat searched for a place to put his front paws. All he could reach were the metal piano strings. He pressed his paws against them as a test. They cut into his paw pads quite a bit, but he thought they would be plenty sturdy to hold his weight for a few seconds. He felt around and found footing for his back paws too.

Stick Cat prepared to push his back up against the bottom of the lid. He took several deep breaths. Right when he was

ready to arch his back and push with all
his strength, he banged the top of his head
against the lid.

He didn't bang his head against the lid
because he slipped.

He banged his head against the lid because
it was at precisely that moment when
the piano came alive with disturbing and
deafening sound.

A series of loud,
banging, off-key
notes echoed from
inside the piano.
Stick Cat backed
himself out as fast
as he could. His

ears rang, and he fell backward off the piano.
He was able to right himself in midair and
land on all four paws, but the impact still
hurt.

He looked up at the piano.

Edith was walking—well, really bounding—
left and right on the keyboard. Her paws
landed between black and white keys,
making an ear-splitting cacophony of sound.

"Edith!" Stick Cat yelled. He rubbed his ears.

She heard him between notes and made a final pounce in the middle of the keyboard—a sort of grand finale of badness.

"Yes, Stick Cat," she said. "What can I do for you?"

"What are you doing?!" Stick Cat yelled. He had not removed his paws from his ears fully—uncertain whether she might bounce up and down on the keys again.

"I thought you might like some musical accompaniment for your rescue," Edith said. "This is kind of a big deal, you know. Cats don't usually rescue humans. It's all quite dramatic. So I thought some really stirring music would add a bit of flair to the whole affair. You know, add a little tension and excitement to the entire situation."

By this time, Edith had hopped down from the piano, and Stick Cat felt comfortable enough to remove his paws from his ears.

"That was very thoughtful of you" was all Stick Cat could think to say. "But I really don't need any more tension or excitement right now."

"Are you sure?" Edith asked. "Remember, I come from a long line of musical performers. Would you like it more if I sang along instead of playing the piano?"

"No," Stick Cat answered immediately. "What I would really like is some help lifting this lid up a few inches so Mr. Music can slide his arms out."

"Well, why didn't you say so?" Edith said. After a moment of consideration, she added, "Maybe I could play something after the big rescue. Something real loud and celebratory."

"Maybe so."

With that, they both hopped up to where Stick Cat had been before.

"Once I squeeze inside and get into position, you come in right next to me," Stick Cat instructed. "Together, maybe we'll have enough strength to lift the lid up for Mr. Music to get his arms out."

Stick Cat climbed into the piano and got into the same position. He called back to Edith, "Okay, I'm good! Now you come in next to me."

Stick Cat was sandwiched in there pretty tightly himself—almost as tightly as Mr. Music's arms were. So he really couldn't turn his head and see Edith as she came in.

He did hear some panting and grunting.

"Are you coming?" he called.

He felt her push and nudge herself against his side outside of the piano.

"How's it going out there?"

There was no answer from Edith. But there was more panting and grunting.

"Can you hurry? This sure isn't very comfortable."

Then total stillness and total silence.

"Edith?"

After a few seconds, she answered. "Yes, Stick Cat?"

"Are you coming?"

"No."

"Why not?"

"I can't fit, all right?" she huffed. "I'm too chubby."

Stick Cat could not help but smile. He had

never heard Edith say anything about herself that wasn't totally flattering. But now, in this tough situation, she had to admit this fact to herself.

"You are not," Stick Cat said. "Don't even think such a thing."

"I am." She sighed. Her voice now quavered a bit. "I'm fat. *P-H-A-T*. Fat!"

Stick Cat knew he had to deal with Edith's

self-doubt issues now. But he also knew that he had to help Mr. Music most of all. He thought for a second or two and then spoke.

"I won't hear any more of this, Edith. I really won't," he called back to her from inside the piano. "You might be a little big boned is all. And besides, if you weren't a little bit bigger, you wouldn't be able to project your voice so nicely when you sing. And that would really be a shame for all of us within hearing distance. A terrible shame."

Edith did not respond.

"To not be able to hear that voice come out loud and clear from your big-boned body— why, that would be just awful," he added. "If you were just some skinny fur-and-bones feline, you couldn't sing as loud as you can now. Imagine depriving the world of that sound. Just imagine! That would be awful."

There was still more silence.

But only for twelve seconds.

And then Edith said, "That really would be a shame, wouldn't it?"

"Yes, it certainly would."

"Humph!" Edith grunted. "I *like* my big bones. And I *like* my singing voice!"

"Good for you."

"You made me feel so

much better, Stick Cat," she said. There was true gratitude in her voice. "Thank you."

"No problem," answered Stick Cat. "Now scoot back a bit. I'm going to try to lift this by myself and then—"

"You know what I'm going to do, Stick Cat?" Edith interrupted. "Just as a thank-you to you?"

"What?"

"I'm going to sing something really inspirational right now," she declared. "Something to give you real hope and joy as you push that piano lid up. That's what I'm going to do!"

"No! No!" Stick Cat exclaimed quickly.

"That's okay. Not now."

"Why not?"

"Umm," Stick Cat said, and paused. "I want you to save all your singing stamina for when we get home after this successful rescue. That's when we'll need a great victory song."

Again there was silence behind him for a few seconds.

Then Edith said, "Sounds like a plan."

Stick Cat took a few deep breaths and twisted his paws to make sure he had a firm footing.

"Are you going to push now or what?" Edith called. "I'm getting kind of bored out here."

"Yes," Stick Cat called. "I'm going to push now."

He gathered his strength, took a deep inhale of air, and pushed with all his power. He pressed his back up against the bottom of the piano lid as hard as he could.

It didn't budge.

Chapter 10

EDITH SITS DOWN

Stick Cat pushed up as hard as he could a second time.

And a third time.

The piano lid did not move at all.

Realizing it was no use, Stick Cat withdrew himself from the piano. His back hurt terribly for a moment. He twisted and stretched to try to loosen his muscles.

"I can't lift it," Stick Cat whispered. He was exhausted from the effort. "We're going to have to think of something else."

"Are you sure an inspirational song by yours truly wouldn't help?" asked Edith. "I promise to sing as loud as I possibly can."

"No," Stick Cat said quickly. The stretching had helped. He started to feel better. "Even something as unique as that sound wouldn't be able to make a difference. It's just too heavy."

"It almost seemed like you were trying to help me," Mr. Music said to Stick Cat. He looked weary from standing so long in one position. His eyes were sad and tired. And his voice sounded weak and raspy. "Is that what you were doing? Or am I starting to hallucinate from all of this? You are real, aren't you?"

Stick Cat came closer and rubbed his side against Mr. Music's right bicep.

"Good," Mr. Music said, and smiled at Stick Cat. "I don't know if you were trying to lift that lid or not, but it's no use. That thing weighs over two hundred pounds. I can barely prop it up myself sometimes."

Stick Cat moved to Mr. Music's other arm and rubbed against the left bicep.

"That feels really good," said Mr. Music. "I think I'm beginning to lose the circulation in my arms. I figured someone at the piano shop would wonder where I was by now. But I'm starting to think that maybe they won't. I called Tony and left a message saying I'd be a little late. I don't even know if he got it. I came straight up here instead of stopping in the shop first. Nobody knows I'm here, little kitty."

Stick Cat gave each of Mr. Music's arms another gentle rub with his side and jumped down to the bench and then down to the floor.

"He's such a nice man," Stick Cat said to

Edith. He paced back and forth near the bench. "We just *have* to think of another way."

"Maybe the problem is the direction in which we're trying to get him out," suggested Edith.

Stick Cat was willing to listen to any idea— mainly because he was having trouble coming up with one of his own. "What do you mean?"

"Well, we're thinking that he has to get his arms out the way they went in," Edith started to explain. "But maybe we could push him farther and farther into the piano until he is all the way inside."

Stick Cat said nothing—primarily because he

could think of nothing to say. This prompted
Edith to continue explaining her idea.

"Once he's all the way inside the piano,
then we can go underneath and scratch and
chew a hole through the bottom. Then he'd
just fall out. End of problem."

"You think we could chew and scratch a
human-size hole in the bottom of a piano?"

"Sure, why not?"

Stick Cat nodded. "Okay, let's keep that plan in mind, and we'll use it if we don't come up with something better."

"Do you honestly think we can come up with something better than chewing a hole through the bottom of the piano?"

Stick Cat paused a moment. Then he said, "I'm just saying maybe we can."

Edith nodded. And Stick Cat began to think even harder.

It was not long before Edith spoke again. "Okay, if we're not going to chew him out from the bottom, maybe we could break the lid from the top."

"Excuse me?" asked Stick Cat. You couldn't really tell if he was so deep in thought himself that he didn't hear Edith—or if he couldn't believe what he just heard.

"We break the lid from the top. It shatters, and he gets his arms out. Simple."

"And how do we break the lid?"

"Any number of ways," Edith answered casually. This all seemed quite obvious to her, you could tell. "We find a way to drop a really heavy object on it. Or we get up there and jump up and down as high as we can. Or we find a sledgehammer and bash on the lid until it breaks. Whatever. There are a million ways."

"But wouldn't that crush Mr. Music's arms?" Stick Cat asked.

Edith sort of pulled her head back. Again,
she seemed astonished at Stick Cat's
question. She said, "Well, of course it would
crush his arms."

"I don't want to do that!"

"Look, Stick Cat," Edith said calmly. "You

asked me for ideas to help Mr. Music out of the piano. You *didn't* ask me for ideas to get him out without shattering his bones to bits."

Stick Cat looked down to the concrete floor and shook his head back and forth ever so slightly. Eventually he lifted his head and said, "I guess I should have mentioned that."

"Umm, ye—ee—ah," Edith said. "I guess you should have."

"We'll keep that plan in mind too," Stick Cat told Edith.

Now, you could tell Edith didn't like it when Stick Cat refused to adopt her most excellent plans. She sighed a lot and shook her head every now and then. Her frustration seemed to grow and grow while Stick Cat continued to pace and think.

Edith finally stopped sighing long enough to say, "Well, if you aren't going to use any of my great ideas, then I'm just going to sit down and wait for you to come up with one of your own."

She plopped down in frustration.

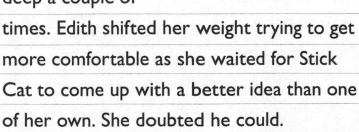

Stick Cat continued to pace. Mr. Music sighed low and deep a couple of times. Edith shifted her weight trying to get more comfortable as she waited for Stick Cat to come up with a better idea than one of her own. She doubted he could.

This pacing and sighing and sitting went on for about thirty seconds more.

That's when Edith did a most peculiar thing. And she screamed the strangest thing Stick Cat had ever heard anyone—cat or human—say.

Edith jumped up from where she sat. She ran in circles and stretched her head back to look at her tail.

She screamed, "My butt is talking! My butt is talking!! MY BUTT IS TALKING!!!"

Chapter 11

ANSWERING THE CALL

Do you know what butt dialing is?
Sometimes people call it pocket dialing.

When someone sits down and accidentally
presses a button on a cell phone in their
pocket, it's called butt dialing. They call
someone by mistake. Or maybe someone's
keys bump against a button on a cell phone,
and it dials someone accidentally.

It happens all the time.
And when the person
who owns the phone
hears a voice coming

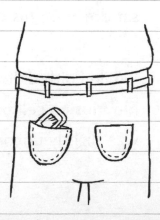

out of their pocket, they reach in and get it and say something like this: "Oh, I'm sorry. I must have butt dialed you."

Well, this is sort of what happened with Edith.

She sat on Mr. Music's cell phone and butt dialed.

Literally.

When she plopped down to wait for Stick Cat to come up with a far-inferior idea to get Mr. Music unstuck from the piano, she sat down on his cell phone.

While Edith didn't know she sat on Mr. Music's cell phone, she did know it was slightly uncomfortable. So she shifted

her weight to change her position. And
when she shifted her weight to change her
position, Edith butt dialed.

She pressed two buttons
on Mr. Music's cell phone.

Do you know what the
two buttons were?

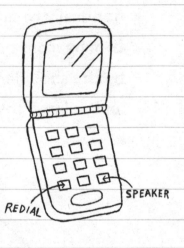

The redial button and the
speaker button.

When someone answered the phone and
it came through the speaker, Edith jumped
up and yelled, "My butt is talking! My butt is
talking!! MY BUTT IS TALKING!!!"

And while Edith didn't recognize what had
happened, Mr. Music instantly did. And

when Mr. Music instantly did, Stick Cat understood what happened too.

He leaped to where Edith was circling frantically to find out where the voice was coming from on her body. He grabbed her by the shoulders, calmed her spinning ways, and pointed toward Mr. Music.

"Max? Max? Are you there?" came the voice from the phone. Apparently, Mr. Music's name was Max.

Mr. Music stretched his neck, turning his head as far as possible to project his voice toward the cell phone down on the floor. "Tony! Tony! It's me!" he yelled. "Whatever you do, don't hang up!"

"I can barely hear you, Max" came Tony's voice from the phone. "You sound far away. I got your message. You said you'd be a little late. Do you need to stay home the whole day?"

"No!" Mr. Music yelled. There was the tiniest hint of desperation in his voice. "No, I'm already here, Tony. I'm up on the twenty-third floor. I got a problem up here—and I need your help!"

"Twenty-third floor?"

"Twenty-third floor!" yelled Mr. Music. "I'm okay. But I do need you to hurry."

"Let me take care of this customer real quick, then I'll close the shop and come up," Tony said. His talking got faster—you could tell he was going to hurry. And then the call ended with a click and a buzz.

Stick Cat smiled the biggest smile he had ever smiled. Mr. Music was going to be okay after all. Mr. Music rested his head sort of sideways on his shoulder. It was clear that a combination of exhaustion and relief had overcome him. He smiled slightly.

"You did it!" Stick Cat said to Edith. "You saved Mr. Music!"

Edith's eyes opened wide. She had put all the pieces together and just now understood what had happened. She said, "Well, of course I did. I'm Edith."

Stick Cat pointed toward the window. He knew they had to get out of there before Mr. Music's coworker arrived. He didn't think there was much danger, but he didn't want them to be mistaken for strays and taken away or something. He couldn't bear the thought of being separated from Goose.

"Come on," he said urgently. He rubbed up once more against Mr. Music's pants leg.

"You're a good kitty," Mr. Music whispered, but didn't open his eyes. "If you're really there."

Stick Cat purred and then turned toward the window, preparing to sprint. "We have to get back. Fast!"

Edith heard the urgency in his voice and turned to race back to the window as well.

But something stopped Stick Cat just then.

"Oh, no," he said quietly, and held completely still.

"What is it, Stick Cat?"

It wasn't Mr. Music saying something—he appeared too tired even to speak anymore. It wasn't a sound. It wasn't a movement. It wasn't the dangerous prospect of crossing back using the clothesline.

Do you know what it was that had Stick Cat so concerned?

It was a smell.

"What is it, Stick Cat?" asked Edith again.

"Mrs. O'Mahoney," he whispered.

"What about her?"

"She's baking bread."

Chapter 12

DING!

Stick Cat could smell the aroma of freshly made bread in the air. Mrs. O'Mahoney was baking. And when Mrs. O'Mahoney baked, she always wore her apron.

They sprinted to the window, but Stick Cat already knew what they would find.

There was no apron on the line.

NO APRON

Far across the alley, Stick Cat could see Mrs. O'Mahoney in the kitchen window. She had just taken a sheet of four freshly baked bread loaves out of the oven. After she pushed another tray of four doughy loaves into the oven to bake, she left the kitchen.

And as Stick Cat had guessed, Mrs. O'Mahoney was wearing the apron.

"Excellent!" Edith said, recognizing the dilemma.

"What's excellent?!" Stick Cat asked. "The apron's gone!"

"We can go back to my idea about grabbing two pigeons by the legs and flying across," Edith explained. "I've always liked that idea."

"Okay, sure," Stick Cat replied, and began to reel the clothespin bag over to their side as fast as he could. He glanced toward Mr. Music at the piano. He still stood there, of course. His eyes were closed and his head rested against his shoulder. He looked incredibly tired, but also relieved to know that help was on the way. Stick Cat took comfort in that—and refocused his concentration.

He knew there was no choice—and no time: they would have to use the clothespin bag hanging on the line. It was much smaller than the apron pocket and full of clothespins. He concentrated on reeling it across. To Edith he said, "Let me know when you see two pigeons flying close enough to jump out and grab."

"I'm on it," Edith said, and got into her ready-to-leap position on the ledge. She snapped her head back and forth to look for incoming pigeons.

It took only a moment for Stick Cat to reel the bag halfway across.

"No pigeons," Edith said to update Stick Cat.

"Keep looking," Stick Cat said as he

retrieved the bag the rest of the way. As soon as he did, he began to empty out all the clothespins. He had to make room in the bag for them to get across. The bag was filled all the way to the top. He piled as many clothespins as he could on the ledge, but there wasn't much room—and he had to be careful. He didn't want any of them to drop down to the street. He knew if one fell from twenty-three floors up, it might hurt somebody on the sidewalk. He also knew it might draw attention to them—and he certainly didn't want that.

"No pigeons," Edith said, providing another update.

"Keep looking," Stick Cat repeated.

When he ran out of room on the window

ledge, Stick Cat began to clasp the remaining clothespins to himself. They pinched his skin, but not too badly. And he was truly in too big of a hurry to care anyway.

Edith, of course, was unaware of any of this. She was far too busy scanning the area for incoming pigeons.

Stick Cat removed the final clothespin and clasped it onto one of his ears.

Edith said, "No pigeons."

"Forget it," Stick Cat said loudly enough to get her attention.

She turned to him and opened her eyes wide at the sight. She stared at him and backed away as far as she could on the

ledge. With fear in her voice, Edith asked, "Did the clothespins attack you?"

"No," Stick Cat explained quickly. "I had to put them somewhere to make room in the bag."

Edith relaxed immediately and said, "You look ridiculous."

"I'm sure I do. But I have a question for you," he said, and smiled. "Do you want to go for another ride?"

Edith didn't take the time to answer. She leaped from the ledge and into the clothespin bag. This time Stick Cat didn't protest at how quickly—and how dangerously—Edith jumped into the bag. He knew there was very little time.

It was far less roomy than the apron pocket, and Stick Cat could tell immediately there would not be space for them both. Mr. Music's coworker was bound to get to the twenty-third floor soon. Stick Cat had to move fast.

As he yanked and reeled the line with his paws to begin Edith's journey across, he shouted instructions to her.

"When you get over there, I'll reel the bag
back," he called. There was true desperation
in his voice. "When I get into the bag, you
reel me across, okay?"

"Okay, sure," Edith said in a way that kind
of made you think she was distracted. Then
the clothespin bag started to sway back and
forth on the line and she yelled, "Wa-hoo!"

Stick Cat's arms and paws never worked so fast as they did getting Edith across that alley. As soon as the bag bumped against Mrs. O'Mahoney's ledge, Edith jumped out. And when Stick Cat saw that she had firm footing, he pulled the bag back as fast as he could. His arms started to throb and hurt, but he kept churning them over and over.

When the bag was about halfway back, Stick Cat heard a sound.

It was a single sound.

Ding!

Ding!

He had heard that sound many times before from Goose's apartment. It seemed to come from out in the hallway of their apartment building. But this time it came from inside the piano factory.

You probably know what it was, right?

It was an elevator getting ready to open.

But Stick Cat had never seen an elevator
before. He probably rode one once when
Goose brought him home as a kitten, but he
didn't remember that at all.

So think about this: if you didn't know what
an elevator was and then suddenly you
heard that sound—*ding!*—and a wall opened
up and somebody stepped out of the wall, it
would be pretty strange, right? And maybe
even a little bit scary, right?

That's exactly what happened to Stick
Cat. There was the *ding!* sound. The wall

opened up. And Tony, Mr. Music's friend and coworker from the piano store, stepped out.

Stick Cat found it all very, very scary. He turned on the ledge, and saw that the empty bag was still four or five feet away.

He aimed for the opening at the top of the bag. He pushed off with both back feet and flew through the air.

Stick Cat missed his target.

Chapter 13

STICK CAT IS NOT TALKING ABOUT EATING PEAS

Stick Cat did not land in the bag.

About halfway through his jump, he could tell he was going to miss. He forgot there were clothespins clasped to his back paws, and they interfered with his push-off. He was coming at the bag too low.

With sheer and rapid instinct, he pressed his front claws out from his paws and dug them into the side of the bag as fast and as deep as he could.

He grabbed the bottom of the bag—and hung on for dear life.

And hung.

And hung.

And hung some more.

He looked over at Mrs. O'Mahoney's window ledge. Edith was there licking her front left paw. It seemed the ride across in the clothespin bag—the very clothespin bag that Stick Cat now hung from twenty-three floors above the street—

had messed up her fur. And Edith was fixing
this problem while
Stick Cat hung.

And hung.

And hung.

"Edith!" he yelled.

She looked up from the ledge and tilted her
head. Then, as if she suddenly recognized the
danger, she began reeling Stick Cat across.

Stick Cat took one look down to the street.
He just couldn't help himself. The street
was so skinny. There was a red siren turning
on top of a parked police car. The cement
truck was still there and so was the broken
streetlight and the wrecked car. The whole

scene seemed to be waving, wobbling, and melting in his vision.

"Do not look down again," Stick Cat whispered to himself. He lifted his head and stared right up at the bottom of the bag as he made his way slowly across the alley.

Until he stopped moving.

Edith had stopped reeling.

"Stick Cat?" she yelled.

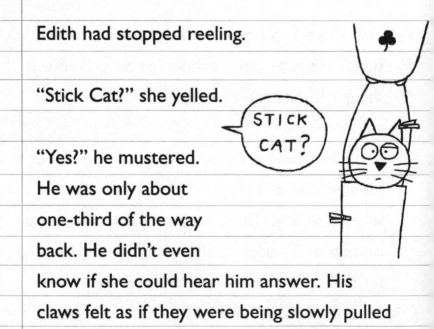

"Yes?" he mustered. He was only about one-third of the way back. He didn't even know if she could hear him answer. His claws felt as if they were being slowly pulled from his paws. It was a terrible feeling.

"Do you think we could play StareDown when you get here?" she called.

"Sure. That's fine," he yelled back.

He started moving again. Stick Cat closed his eyes and concentrated all his energy on his claws. He tried to keep them perfectly still as they dug into the material. It seemed that when the bag rocked a little or when the line jerked a little, his claws would rip into the clothespin bag material and tear it just a fraction.

He definitely didn't want that to happen anymore.

RRRIP!

RRRIP!

He stopped again.

He opened his eyes.

He was perhaps halfway across now.

"Stick Cat?"

He began to understand that it was quite difficult for Edith to do two things—reel the clothesline and talk—at the same time. He felt exhausted. He took a quick inhale of air and called back, "Yes?"

"Maybe we could get some rolled-up socks out of Goose's drawer again," Edith suggested. "I forgot how fun that was."

"Okay," Stick Cat called. He began to lose feeling in his front paws. He answered quickly, hoping to get moving again, "Sure."

But he didn't move again.

"Stick Cat, are you even listening to me?" Edith yelled.

Stick Cat nodded. He didn't want to call to Edith anymore. Even that simple thing made the bag swing a little.

"What did I say then?" Edith asked.

He had to speak now. "StareDown and Goose's socks."

"Oh, good! You *were* listening," Edith said. There was real pleasure in her voice. "I just can't stand it when someone isn't paying attention."

Stick Cat started moving again.

For a moment.

Then he wasn't.

"Stick Cat?"

He nodded.

"Why are you hanging like that? I think it would be much more comfortable if you rode *inside* the bag like I did."

Now his shoulders ached. He felt his claws losing their grip. He tried to flex and push them in farther, but he didn't want any more material to tear. It was a delicate balance.

He took a deep inhale of air, but his voice came out weak and whispery when he asked, "Could you reel me the rest of the way home, please?"

"What's that?"

"Reel me in, please," he repeated. He risked turning his head a little to look at Edith. Maybe if she saw the concern on his face, she would speed things up.

Edith was on the ledge. Her head was tilted at an odd angle—as if she was trying to figure something out. "You really like to eat peas?" she called. "Is that what you said?"

"Reel me in, please," he tried to call again. But his voice was even weaker.

"What a strange time to be thinking about eating peas," Edith said. She talked to herself as much as to Stick Cat. She did start pulling on the clothesline again, however. "I mean, look at you out there. Hanging from that thing, and all you can think about is eating peas."

Stick Cat said absolutely nothing in response. He closed his eyes and held his body as still as he could. He concentrated all his energy on his claws and keeping them clenched into the material.

And then he felt something.

It was Mrs. O'Mahoney's ledge. He had made it.

He reached for the ledge one leg at a time,

releasing his claws from the clothespin bag
carefully.

He sat down on the ledge next to Edith and
began to take the clothespins off his body
and drop them into the bag, which still hung
on the line. As he did this, Edith said, "That
really hurts the paws."

Stick Cat nodded. "You wouldn't believe
how much," he said, and gingerly rubbed his
paws together. "I thought my claws were
going to rip right out. I don't think I could
have held on too much longer."

"Humph," Edith said, and held up her own
paws. "I wasn't talking about *your* paws, Mr.
Man. I was talking about mine. Pulling you
over here wasn't so easy, you know!"

"Oh," Stick Cat said in quick acknowledgment. By this time, he had removed all the clothespins from his fur. "Well, of course you were. Thank you for getting me across."

"It was nothing." Edith sighed and casually stroked the top of her head from front to back.

"And so fast too," Stick Cat added.

"Yes," Edith said. "Let's be honest, Stick Cat. It's really quite lucky that you have me around."

Stick Cat smiled. "I know."

"Come on!" Edith said, and jumped from Mrs. O'Mahoney's ledge to Stick Cat's. "Let's play StareDown."

This time Stick Cat jumped right behind her to his own window ledge.

And he landed perfectly.

Chapter 14

"I DON'T WANT TO COUNT THAT HIGH"

Stick Cat was exhausted. And he decided to admit it to Edith right away.

"Edith," he said. "I don't think I can play StareDown or play with Goose's socks right now. I'm really tired."

Edith nodded in understanding, and Stick Cat was thankful for that.

"I'm kind of tired too," she said. "I'm not too tired to sing you that victory song though. Do you still want me to do that?"

She began to hum a little as a warm-up. At least, Stick Cat thought she was humming. She might have had something stuck in her throat. He couldn't quite tell.

"No, that's okay," Stick Cat said as fast and politely as he could.

"All right," Edith said. She stopped humming and shrugged. She didn't seem to mind. After helping Stick Cat push the window back down so that it was open just a few inches, she added, "Besides, there are still some breakfast dishes in the sink back at my place. And I'm pretty hungry."

EDITH'S SNACKS

"Great," Stick Cat said. He was already curling up on the inside windowsill—his favorite spot. Now that he knew Mr. Music was safe and Edith was going home, sleepiness came on fast. He would close the bathroom cabinet door and clean up from their treasure hunt after a quick snooze. "See you tomorrow then. Thanks for all your help rescuing Mr. Music."

"No problem at all," answered Edith. She stopped halfway across the living room and looked back over her shoulder at Stick Cat. There was a genuine sense of accomplishment on her face. "Next time there's an emergency, just let me know, and I'll sit down and save the day."

Stick Cat smiled and closed his eyes.

Do you know how you fall asleep really quickly and deeply after a day in which you've accomplished something important and satisfying? Maybe you finished a big chore at home—like cleaning out the whole garage or something. Maybe you got a good grade on a test at school.

Well, that's what happened to Stick Cat.

The fact that he had helped rescue Mr. Music made him feel so proud—and so sleepy.

Complete contentment washed over his whole body as he settled into his most comfortable and cozy sleeping position on the windowsill.

He didn't fall asleep though.

Do you know why?

It's because Edith called to him from the bathroom.

"Stick Cat!" she yelled. "I'm stuck again!"

He hopped down from his favorite perch and started across the living room.

Edith wanted to make sure she heard him. "Stick Cat! Stick Cat!!"

"I'm coming," he called when he was almost to the bathroom. He had heard her just fine—even though her head was through the hole and in her own apartment now.

When he got to the bathroom, he peeked into the cabinet under the sink and saw only Edith's tail end.

"Stick Cat!"

"I'm right here," he said upon entering the cabinet.

"Oh, I couldn't tell. I can't see behind me," Edith explained. "Someone has been making the hole smaller again."

"I see that."

"I'm really wedged in here," Edith grunted.
"We're going to have to get me unstuck
again."

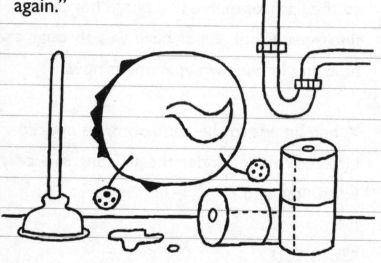

Stick Cat smiled. "I don't mean to be
repetitive," he said. "But by 'we,' you mean
'me,' right?"

Edith said nothing for almost a full minute.
And Stick Cat decided to wait until she
spoke.

Finally, she responded.

"Look, Stick Cat. This big-boned butt of mine just saved Mr. Music by sitting down on exactly the right spot and hitting exactly the right buttons on his phone. So don't you give me any grief."

"Okay, okay," Stick Cat said, and smiled.

"Just give me a good push," requested Edith. "I should pop through if you're strong enough."

Stick Cat thought about this for a few seconds. After this consideration, he said, "So, if you don't pop through, it's because I'm not strong enough? It's not for any other reason?"

"What exactly are you saying?!" Edith said immediately. "What are you implying?"

"Nothing, nothing," said Stick Cat. He pointed his left shoulder and braced himself to push against Edith. "You count to three and then I'll start pushing, okay?"

"No, not okay!"

"Why not?"

"Because I don't want to count so high, that's why!"

"You don't want to count as high as three? Really!?"

"Just start shoving, okay? Forget the whole counting thing. Just start shoving."

And that's exactly what Stick Cat did.

He pushed his left shoulder into Edith's hind quarters. After a few seconds, she popped through the hole and was released into her own bathroom cabinet—and her own apartment. She peeked back through the hole at Stick Cat. She looked a little guilty for some reason.

"Thanks," Edith said. "Maybe I'll scratch at the hole tomorrow and make it a little bigger."

"I'll help you," replied Stick Cat.

And with that, Stick Cat closed the cabinet door in the bathroom and headed back to his favorite sleeping spot.

Chapter 15

ENCORE

Finally, it was time to sleep.

Stick Cat curled up on the windowsill. He glanced down at the street twenty-three floors below and saw a tow truck taking the cement truck away. He glanced sideways and saw Mrs. O'Mahoney's arms reaching out of her kitchen window next door to tie her apron back onto the clothesline. He could smell the warm baking bread.

And then he looked across the alley to the piano factory.

Mr. Music sat on the
piano bench. He rubbed
his arms in an attempt to
reinvigorate the circulation
in them. His coworker,
Tony, was now gone.
Stick Cat figured
that while he and
Edith were crossing
the alley and getting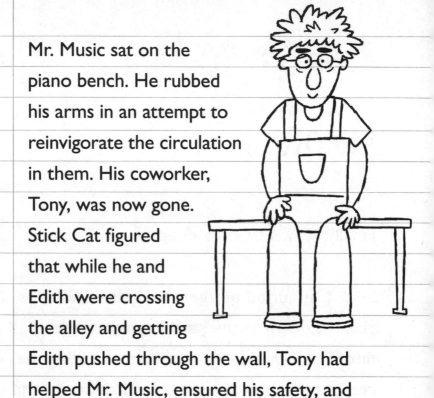
Edith pushed through the wall, Tony had
helped Mr. Music, ensured his safety, and
disappeared back into that strange wall.

Knowing that Mr. Music was safe made
Stick Cat feel even sleepier.

Stick Cat closed his eyes.

But he didn't fall asleep.

Do you know why?

It wasn't because Edith got stuck in the wall
again. She was, by this time, happily on her
own kitchen counter, licking the breakfast
dishes in the sink.

No, this was something altogether different.

You see, when Stick Cat closed his eyes,
Mr. Music got up from the bench to close
the piano factory's windows. And when he
started to close the last window—the one
directly across from Stick Cat's apartment—
Mr. Music lifted his head and looked at the
apartment building.

And he saw Stick Cat on the inside ledge of
that window.

He stopped and stared at Stick Cat for nearly thirty seconds.

And then Mr. Music opened that window as high as he could push it. He walked back to the black grand piano and sat down on the bench. He propped the lid open very, very carefully. Mr. Music stretched his arms, rubbed them again, and cracked his knuckles.

And then Mr. Music began to play.

It was a slow and melancholy tune—almost like a lullaby. It mixed softly and quietly with the sound patterns of traffic drifting up from the street.

Stick Cat had never heard anything so quietly beautiful. He opened his eyes one time only—to ensure that he wasn't dreaming. He wanted to know that it was Mr. Music playing for him.

When he saw that it was, Stick Cat closed his eyes again.

He listened as long as he could.

Until he fell asleep.

THE END

Tom Watson is the author of the Stick Dog series. There are currently five books in that series—and more to come.

He lives in Chicago with his wife, daughter, and son. He also has a dog, as you could probably guess. The dog is a Labrador-Newfoundland mix. Tom says he looks like a Labrador with a bad perm. He wanted to name the dog "Put Your Shirt On" (please don't ask why), but he was outvoted by his family. The dog's name is Shadow. Shadow gives Tom lots of ideas for the Stick Dog series.

Tom Watson is also the author of the new Stick Cat series. This story is the first in that series.

Tom does not have a cat. So his ideas for the Stick Cat series come from a whole different place. He's not sure where that place is exactly, but he knows it's kind of strange there.

While he has your attention, Tom would like to make one thing perfectly clear: There are not going to be any other stick animal books.

There won't be a Stick Monkey, for instance. Or Stick Chicken (even though that's fun to say). There will be no Stick Goat, Stick Pig, or Stick Donkey books. A Stick Cow story could be interesting, but he's not doing it. Don't count on any Stick Fish, Stick Rooster, or Stick Giraffe (even though that would be neat to draw) books.

He's having plenty of fun just with dogs and cats.

Visit him online at stickdogbooks.com!

Also available as an ebook.